Put Beginning Readers on the Right Track with
ALL ABOARD READING™

The All Aboard Reading series is especially for beginning readers. Written by noted authors and illustrated in full color, these are books that children really and truly *want* to read—books to excite their imagination, tickle their funny bone, expand their interests, and support their feelings. With four different reading levels, All Aboard Reading lets you choose which books are most appropriate for your children and their growing abilities.

Picture Readers—for Ages 3 to 6
Picture Readers have super-simple texts with many nouns appearing as rebus pictures. At the end of each book are 24 flash cards—on one side is the rebus picture; on the other side is the written-out word.

Level 1—for Preschool through First Grade Children
Level 1 books have very few lines per page, very large type, easy words, lots of repetition, and pictures with visual "cues" to help children figure out the words on the page.

Level 2—for First Grade to Third Grade Children
Level 2 books are printed in slightly smaller type than Level 1 books. The stories are more complex, but there is still lots of repetition in the text and many pictures. The sentences are quite simple and are broken up into short lines to make reading easier.

Level 3—for Second Grade through Third Grade Children
Level 3 books have considerably longer texts, use harder words and more complicated sentences.

All Aboard for happy reading!

Library of Congress Cataloging-in-Publication Data

Bergen, Lara
    Washington Irving's Rip Van Winkle / retold by Lara Bergen ; illustrated by Donald Cook.
       p.   cm. — (All aboard reading)
    Summary: A retelling of the tale in which a man who sleeps for twenty years in the Catskill Mountains wakes to a much-changed world.
    [1. Catskill Mountains Region (N.Y.)—Fiction.   2. New York (State)—Fiction.]
    I. Irving, Washington, 1783–1859. Rip Van Winkle. II. Cook, Donald, ill. III. Title.
    IV. Series.
    PZ7.B44985Was   1997
    [E]—dc20   96-24335
                                                                   CIP

ISBN 0-448-41733-2 (GB)   A B C D E F G H I J   AC

ISBN 0-448-41136-9 (pbk.)   A B C D E F G H I J

ALL
ABOARD
READING™

Level 2
Grades 1-3

WASHINGTON IRVING'S
Rip Van Winkle

**Retold by
Lara Bergen**

**Illustrated by
Donald Cook**

Grosset & Dunlap • New York

In a little town

at the foot of a big mountain

lived a jolly man.

His name was Rip Van Winkle.

Everybody in town knew Rip.

And everybody liked him.

Rip was fun.

He liked to fish

and play with the children.

But most of all,

Rip liked to sit by the Town Hall

and tell stories.

"Do I have a story for you!"

he would say.

Rip told all kinds of stories—

silly stories,

and fairy stories,

and scary stories.

But the story Rip liked best

was about the little men—

the little men who lived

on the mountain.

"They wear funny little clothes.

And they have long, long beards.

I have never seen them.

But I have heard them,"

Rip would say.

"They like to go bowling.

CRASH! BOOM!

Down go the pins.

We think it is thunder.

But it is not.

It is the little men!"

Of course,

no one believed Rip's stories.

But they liked to listen just the same.

Rip spent a <u>lot</u> of time telling stories.

But he spent only a <u>little</u> time

working on his farm.

Rip's wife was always mad at him.

"This farm is a mess!"

Dame Van Winkle yelled.

"Get to work, Rip!"

"Yes, dear," Rip said.

"But first I have a story for you."

"No! No! No stories!"

his wife yelled.

"There is work to do!"

Rip sighed.

Dame Van Winkle was no fun.

"I know," Rip said.

"I will catch us some dinner."

Rip picked up his fishing pole.

And he started up the mountain.

Soon he found a spot by a stream.

Rip was all ready to fish.

But then he saw a very funny sight.

It was a funny little man.

He wore funny little clothes.

And he had a long, long beard.

He was rolling a cider barrel

up, up, up the mountain.

Now who could this little man be?

Rip put down his pole.

He walked over to the man.

"Need a hand?" Rip asked.

The man did not say yes.

But the man did not say no.

So Rip helped him roll.

Up, up, up

the mountain they went.

Rip tried to talk to the little man.

But his voice was drowned out

by the sound of thunder.

CRASH! BOOM!

At last they came

to the very top of the mountain.

And Rip's eyes grew wide.

What did he see?

Lots of funny little men!

They all wore funny little clothes.

They all had long, long beards.

And they all were . . .

bowling!

"What do you know!" Rip cried.

"My story is true—

every bit!"

He could not wait to tell everyone.

"But first," Rip said,

"I will have some fun."

So he bowled,

and drank cider,

and bowled some more.

Rip had so much fun,

he wore himself out.

"I will sit down just for a moment,"

he told himself.

So he did.

Then Rip fell asleep.

And he kept on sleeping,

and sleeping,

and sleeping.

The next thing Rip knew,

it was morning.

He rubbed his eyes and looked around.

The funny little men were gone.

But Rip did not have time
to look for them.
Not now.
He had to get home.
Fast!
"My wife will have a fit!"
Rip said.

Rip went down the mountain.

At last he came to a field of weeds.

He saw an old house.

It had broken windows and a broken roof.

A broken sign said "Rip Van Winkle".

Was <u>this</u> Rip's farm?

Then where was his family?

Rip rubbed his chin.

Why, his beard was to his belt!

And it was white!

"This is very odd," Rip said.

"Very odd indeed."

But Rip did not have time

to think about his beard.

He had to find his family.

So he set off for town.

The town was not at all the way

Rip remembered it.

The town had new streets.

And the streets had new names.

Even the people were new to Rip.

Rip did not know them.

And they did not know Rip.

The men stared.

The women pointed.

The children laughed.

"Look at that ragged old man!"

they cried.

Even the dogs barked at Rip.

Rip scratched his head.

Was he in some other town?

No.

There was the Town Hall

with its big brass bell.

There were people standing outside.

"Hello, stranger," a young man said.

"May we help you?"

"Er . . . um . . . I am looking

for my family," Rip said.

"Who are you?" a woman asked.

Rip stood up as tall as he could.

"Rip Van Winkle, of course."

The people laughed.

"What's so funny?" Rip asked.

"How can you be Rip Van Winkle?"

the young man asked.

"He is over there."

39

Sure enough,

fast asleep under a tree

was Rip—

another Rip!

"That is Rip Van Winkle,"

the young man said.

"He was named for his father.

The poor man went up the mountain

twenty years ago

and never came down."

Twenty years ago! What was going on?

Rip sat down.

Had the funny little men

put him under a spell?

Had he been asleep for twenty years?

His wife was really going to have a fit!

Rip took a closer look

at the sleeping man.

Yes. It was his son.

"So," Rip said slowly.

"Where is old Rip's wife?"

The young man shook his head.

"She died years ago," he said.

"She got so mad when Rip left,

she had a fit, so they say."

So his wife was dead.

Rip was surprised!

But was he sad?

Well . . .

maybe a little.

"So tell us," the young man said,

"who are you really?"

Rip grinned.

"Do I have a story for you!"

he said.

Of course,

no one believed Rip's story.

But they liked to listen

just the same.